"Room 208. It must be at the other end of the hall."

Timothy, Titus, and Sarah-Jane tiptoed in single file along the dark, empty corridor. They had gone about halfway when they began hearing footsteps behind them that weren't theirs.

Sarah-Jane grabbed Titus, and Titus grabbed Timothy.

Suddenly a book seemed to zoom by itself across the hall. And somewhere nearby, a door slammed shut. . . .

Solve all the Beatitudes Mysteries along with Sarah-Jane, Ti, and Tim:

The Mystery of the Empty School
"Blessed are the meek"

The Mystery of the Candy Box
"Blessed are the merciful"

The Mystery of the Disappearing Papers
"Blessed are the pure in heart"

The Mystery of the Secret Snowman
"Blessed are the peacemakers"

The Mystery of the Golden Pelican
"Blessed are those who mourn"

The Mystery of the Princess Doll
"Blessed are those who are persecuted"

The Mystery of the Hidden Egg
"Blessed are the poor in spirit"

The Mystery of the Clumsy Juggler
"Blessed are those who hunger and thirst for righteousness"

THE MYSTERY OF THE EMPTY SCHOOL

Elspeth Campbell Murphy
Illustrated by Chris Wold Dyrud

Chariot Books™
David C. Cook Publishing Co.

A Wise Owl Book
Published by Chariot Books™,
an imprint of David C. Cook Publishing Co.
David C. Cook Publishing Co., Elgin, Illinois 60120
David C. Cook Publishing Co., Weston, Ontario

THE MYSTERY OF THE EMPTY SCHOOL
© 1989 by Elspeth Campbell Murphy for text and Chris Wold Dyrud
for illustrations.

All rights reserved. Except for brief excerpts for review purposes, no
part of this book may be reproduced or used in any form without
written permission from the publisher.

Cover design by Steve Smith
First printing, 1989
Printed in the United States of America
94 93 92 91 90   5 4 3

Library of Congress Cataloging-in-Publication Data
Murphy, Elspeth Campbell.
   The mystery of the empty school / Elspeth Campbell Murphy;
illustrated by Chris Wold Dyrud.
       p.   cm.—(The Beatitudes mysteries)
   Summary: With the help of a teacher, three cousins investigate
strange happenings at a school and learn the meaning of "Blessed are
the meek, for they will inherit the earth."
   ISBN 1-55513-561-7
   [1. Cousins—Fiction. 2. Mystery and detective stories.
3. Beatitudes—Fiction.] I. Dyrud, Chris Wold, ill. II. Title.
III. Series: Murphy, Elspeth Campbell. Beatitudes mysteries.
PZ7.S3636Wh   1989
[Fic]—dc19   88-35240
                                                         CIP
                                                          AC

CONTENTS

1 Back-to-School Blues   7

2 Stevenson Elementary   9

3 Ghostly Happenings   15

4 In the Supply Room   18

5 Good Adventure   22

6 Funny Weird   28

7 What Stuff?   33

8 Trapped!   38

9 The Search   40

10 The Best Yet   45

"Blessed are the meek,
for they will inherit the earth."
Matthew 5:5 (NIV)

1
BACK-TO-SCHOOL BLUES

"I *hate* school!" Timothy Dawson declared, jabbing at the perky little balls of cereal that kept bobbing up through the milk in his bowl.

His two visiting cousins, Sarah-Jane Cooper and Titus McKay, looked up quickly to see how their aunt would react to this.

But Timothy's mother took it very calmly— either that or she wasn't awake yet.

"Nonsense, Timothy," she said, pouring herself another cup of coffee. "We go through this every year. You do very well once school gets under way, but you have a hard time saying good-bye to summer."

"It still feels like summer," said Sarah-Jane.

"You can say that again," said Timothy.

In fact, that's how they had gotten to talking

about school in the first place. The cousins had just figured out that Titus and Sarah-Jane didn't have to go back to their schools until after Labor Day. But Timothy's school started next week, when there was still plenty of August left to go. Timothy was pretty mad about that. It helped a *little* bit to remember that he would get out earlier next June. . . .

But just as Timothy was looking forward to next summer already his mother made an announcement. "Today's the day they put up the class lists at school. You three could go over there and find out who Timothy's teacher is going to be."

Timothy groaned and collapsed on the kitchen floor. "I can't take it!" he said. "I have a stomachache! I have a temperature of a hundred and ninety-two!"

But Titus and Sarah-Jane didn't give him any sympathy. Instead, they each grabbed an arm and dragged him off to school.

2
STEVENSON ELEMENTARY

"Well, there it is," said Titus cheerfully as they came up to the corner. "Good old Robert Louis Stevenson Elementary."

"*Bad* old, you mean," muttered Timothy.

Titus said, "It just looks like an ordinary school to me. What's so bad about it?"

"Oh, nothing, I guess," sighed Timothy. "Except it's probably going to be superhard this year. This is the year I go upstairs."

Sarah-Jane said, "I don't know what you're so worried about, Tim. You're smart."

"Yeah, Tim," Titus added. "What are you so scared of? Let's go see who your teacher is."

On the way across the street, they argued about whether it was better to know who your teacher would be before summer started (like

Titus) or not till the first day of school (like Sarah-Jane) or sort of in-between (like Timothy).

They pulled open the big front doors and stepped into the lobby.

Timothy was glad to see that they weren't the only ones there. A few parents and kids were eagerly studying the lists of names on the big bulletin board. And a couple of lower-grade teachers, dressed in T-shirts and jeans, hurried by. They were lugging record players and headphones to their classrooms. But even with some people around, Stevenson Elementary was weirdly quiet.

Timothy took a deep breath and marched over to the bulletin board. Titus and Sarah-Jane didn't even have to push him. In fact, they were the ones who hung back a little.

Mrs. Mason, the principal, was putting the finishing touches on the board. She could just have tacked up the lists, but that wasn't the way Mrs. Mason did things. Instead, she had cut out big construction paper letters that spelled out WELCOME BACK!! in all capital letters with two exclamation points.

Mrs. Mason turned around with a bright smile. "Well, if it isn't Timothy Dawson!"

Timothy knew that the principal prided herself on knowing every single kid in the whole school and even his relatives. She peered closely at Sarah-Jane and Titus. "I don't know you two. Are you new?"

Timothy introduced his cousins and explained that they were just visiting and that their schools didn't start until after Labor Day.

Mrs. Mason declared that starting after

Labor Day was too late, because children were always bored by the end of summer and dying to get back to school.

The cousins glanced at one another. They did not agree with this point of view. But they were too polite—and smart—to make gagging noises.

"Now, let's see," continued Mrs. Mason. "I just this minute put up your class list, Timothy. Where is it? Oh, yes. Mr. Bender, Room 208."

Timothy felt his stomach fall into his shoes. A *man* teacher? He had never had a man teacher before in his whole life. And who was Mr. Bender anyway? He had never even heard of him.

As if reading his mind, Mrs. Mason said, "Mr. Bender is new to Stevenson this year. A very dedicated young man. He came in early to get his classroom ready. So you're in luck, Timothy. You can go right upstairs and meet him now."

Timothy gulped.

"Don't look so scared," ordered Mrs. Mason. "He doesn't bite. Now, run along and say hello."

For an awful moment Timothy thought Mrs. Mason was actually going to pick him up and carry him upstairs. But she gathered her stuff and bustled back into the office.

Titus and Sarah-Jane turned to Timothy. But before they could say anything, an older kid came out from behind the stairway. He sidled up to them and whispered urgently, "I wouldn't do that if I were you."

"Do what?" asked Timothy.

"Go upstairs."

"But Mrs. Mason just told me I have to."

The older boy looked around quickly as if to make sure he wasn't being overheard. Then he leaned closer and spoke quickly. "*She* doesn't want anyone to find out about it. But listen. I used to go here, and I *know*. It's OK during the day when school is going on, right? But not at night. Or on the weekends. And *especially not* during the summer. Got that? You look like nice kids, and I just had to warn you. What they say about this place is *true*. I'm telling you, do *not*—repeat, do *not*—go upstairs!"

The older boy turned to go out the back door

that led to the parking lot. The cousins hurried after him. What in the world was he talking about?

"Wait a minute," said Titus. "You haven't told us anything."

"Yeah," said Timothy. "Why shouldn't we go upstairs?"

The older boy stared back at them. He looked as if he couldn't believe that they didn't know the awful thing he knew. And he looked as if he didn't want to be the one to tell them. But finally he swallowed hard and said, "The upstairs floor of this school is haunted."

3
GHOSTLY HAPPENINGS

Without another word, the boy hunched up his heavy-looking book bag and hurried toward a dark blue station wagon where a teenage girl waited in the driver's seat.

The cousins stared after him.

"*Haunted*!?" Titus gasped. "Did he say *haunted*? Tim, you never told us your school was *haunted*!"

"I never knew," protested Timothy weakly as they turned back to the lobby. They all glanced nervously toward the shadowy stillness at the top of the stairs.

At that moment, Mrs. Mason rapped on the office hallway window, and they jumped about a foot and a half straight up. The principal made shooing motions toward the stairs.

So the three of them reluctantly headed that way. And all the way up they kept saying things like:

"That guy was talking crazy."

"Yeah, who does he think we are? Babies?"

"I don't even believe in ghosts."

"Me neither."

"Me neither."

"Who ever heard of a school being haunted? It's not like it was an old castle or something."

"Yeah. Who ever heard of a haunted school?"

The upstairs hall was dim and still. The cousins spoke in whispers, because when they said something out loud, their voices sounded strangely hollow.

"OK," Timothy murmured. "Let's get this over with. Room 208. It must be at the other end of the hall."

Without even planning to, they tiptoed in single file. They had gone about halfway when they began hearing soft footsteps behind them that weren't theirs.

Sarah-Jane grabbed Titus, and Titus grabbed Timothy. Together they made themselves turn around and look.

The corridor was completely empty.

Then suddenly a book seemed to zoom by itself across the hall. And somewhere nearby, a door slammed shut.

That did it.

The cousins spun around and fled down the hall. They burst into Room 208 in a breathless heap.

4
IN THE SUPPLY ROOM

A young man turned around in surprise from the poster he was tacking to the bulletin board. "Hi," he said, sounding friendly and amused at the same time. "I'm Mr. Bender. Who are you?"

He sounded nice and the room looked safe and normal with its clutter of ordinary school stuff. The cousins relaxed and tried to catch their breath.

"What's the matter?" asked Mr. Bender. "You look as if you've just seen a ghost."

"Well, not exactly," gasped Sarah-Jane. "But we think we *heard* one."

"Yes!" added Titus. "Someone told us that the upstairs part of this school is haunted. But of course we didn't believe it, except now . . ."

His voice trailed off, and he looked a little embarrassed.

"It was probably just nothing," Timothy said, trying to sound casual.

"I'm sure you're right," said his teacher. "This is the first I've heard about Stevenson being haunted. And I think we all agree that there's no such thing as a ghost?"

The cousins nodded solemnly.

"Good," said Mr. Bender, pushing back his light brown hair. "Still, it wouldn't hurt to investigate."

"We're good at that," said Titus.

"We're the T.C.D.C.," said Sarah-Jane.

"What's a 'teesy-deesy'?" asked Mr. Bender.

"It's letters," Timothy explained.

"Capital T.
Capital C.
Capital D.
Capital C.
It stands for the Three Cousins Detective Club."

"Sounds like a great club! Does this mean I have three cousins in my class?"

"No," said Timothy. "Just me. I'm Timothy Dawson, and these are my cousins, Sarah-Jane Cooper and Titus McKay. They're just visiting, and their own schools don't even start until after Labor Day."

Mr. Bender replied, "I wish ours didn't. Somehow it's hard to get going on school when it's still August."

Timothy had already decided that he liked Mr. Bender because of the friendly way his eyes crinkled up at the corners when he smiled. Now he decided he liked Mr. Bender even more because of his sensible views about when school should start.

The cousins followed Mr. Bender out into the hallway. He flipped on the light switches that only janitors and teachers were allowed to touch, and instantly the hallway looked a lot less strange. Also, Mr. Bender was just the right kind of grown-up to have around. He didn't make you feel dumb for being scared, but he still let you know there was nothing to be scared of.

Titus said, "There's the book that came flying across the hall.''

They went over to take a closer look. The book lay splat open on the floor.

Mr. Bender stooped to pick it up. "Hmmm," he said. "*Journeys in Spelling*. Now why would anyone want to throw that on the floor?" His voice sounded serious, but Timothy saw the corner of his mouth twitch.

Titus said, "It could have come from that room across the hall."

They went to take a look.

The room was close to the stairway. And, sure enough, when they opened the door they found a large storeroom filled with art supplies and books for the upper-grade classrooms.

Mr. Bender carefully smoothed out the rumpled page of *Journeys in Spelling* and put it back in its own pile. Then he walked farther back and looked behind the rows of shelves.

Timothy said, "It looks like the book came from this room all right."

"Yes," said Mr. Bender, joining them. "But who threw it? There's no one in here but us."

There was no one in the other rooms, either. Mr. Bender and the cousins checked just to make sure.

Sarah-Jane said, "Whoever threw the book could have gone downstairs while we were in Tim's classroom." And the others agreed.

By this time Timothy, Titus, and Sarah-Jane were getting over their creepy feelings and dying to find out what was going on.

They followed Mr. Bender back to Room 208. Then it was a little awkward, because there was no reason for them to hang around. But they didn't want to leave.

Mr. Bender went back to tacking up the poster, and the cousins went over to take a closer look.

The poster showed a breathtaking photograph of mountain climbers looking out over the whole land spread before them.

"Neat-O," murmured Timothy.

"EXcellent," agreed Titus.

"So cool," said Sarah-Jane.

Timothy thought Mr. Bender looked strong, and he wondered if he climbed mountains in his spare time. Maybe later he would ask.

At the bottom of the poster was a hand-printed caption that said, *Good Adventure to the Disciplined, for the World Belongs to Them.*

"It's a kind of motto of mine," Mr. Bender explained.

Sarah-Jane frowned thoughtfully. "It sounds like it comes from the Bible or something."

"It does," said Mr. Bender. "It's a paraphrase of the Beatitude that says, 'Blessed are the meek, for they will inherit the earth.' The English word 'blessed' means 'happy,' and that's a fine translation. But I like the Spanish better. *Bienaventurados* means 'good adventure.' I think it sounds exciting—as if you're cheering somebody on."

Timothy said, "You mean that saying 'Good adventure to you!' is sort of like saying, 'Way to go!' "

"Exactly!" said Mr. Bender. "The word 'meek' is a fine word, too. But, unfortunately, people think it means 'wimpy' or 'weak.' Actually, 'meekness' just means that a person isn't conceited or bossy. A meek person is someone who's just matter-of-fact about himself or herself and courteous to other people. A meek person has a good attitude."

Sarah-Jane nodded. "I can't stand it when people think they know it all and that they can push other people around."

"Yeah," said Titus. "It's like they think they own the world or something."

"But that's where they're wrong," said Mr. Bender. "The world really belongs to the people who make it a better place. The meek people. The *disciplined* people. Those are the people who work hard. They're humble enough to admit they have a lot to learn. And they're the ones who control themselves even when things go wrong. They're gentle—they care about

24

other people's feelings, too."

Titus excitedly pushed his glasses up on his nose and said, "Hey, guess what! I just made up a new motto: *Blessed are the meek, because they don't act like jerks.*"

Mr. Bender laughed so hard that Timothy felt a little jealous he hadn't thought of it first.

But he forgot about feeling jealous when Mr. Bender said, "Listen, are you kids busy? Because I sure could use some help around here."

The cousins thought that sounded like a great idea. So Mr. Bender got Titus and Sarah-Jane started on projects while Timothy ran downstairs to call his mother.

As soon as Timothy hung up the phone, he saw Mrs. Mason outside the back door, struggling with a load of plants. He ran to open the door for her.

"Thank you so much, Timothy," she said. "And thank you, too, young man." She turned to a boy behind her that Timothy hadn't seen at first. It was the same boy who had told the cousins that the school was haunted.

Mrs. Mason said, "How lucky for me that

you just happened to be passing through the
parking lot at the right time. What is your
name?"

"Um—Dave," the boy said promptly.

"Well, thank you again, Dave. Timothy and
I can manage from here."

When Mrs. Mason's back was turned, the
boy gave Timothy a warning look and shook his
head as if to say, "Are you crazy? What are you
still doing here?"

But when Mrs. Mason turned back to say
good-bye, he just smiled politely and sauntered

away, swinging his book bag up in the air and catching it. Timothy wasn't positive, but he thought he saw the same dark blue station wagon in the parking lot.

There was something strange going on here.

Timothy headed back upstairs. And even though the upstairs hall lights were on, he felt a shiver run up and down his spine.

6
FUNNY WEIRD

Sarah-Jane and Titus were alone in the classroom when Timothy got back. They explained that Mr. Bender had gone downstairs to help another teacher move some bookcases. Maybe it was because they were busy, but Titus and Sarah-Jane seemed to have gotten all over being scared. That made Timothy feel better.

They worked in silence for a while.

Then Sarah-Jane asked, "You know what's funny?"

"Funny ha-ha or funny weird?" Titus asked back.

"Funny weird."

"I don't know. What?"

"That Tim didn't know the school was haunted."

"Oh, not that again," groaned Timothy. "I thought we agreed that the school *isn't* haunted. It's just dumb stories."

"I know," said Sarah-Jane. "But that's just it. If there are stories about Stevenson being haunted, how come you haven't heard any of them? And Mr. Bender hasn't either. Usually when a place is supposed to be haunted, *everybody* knows about it."

Titus said, "So how did that guy downstairs know Stevenson is supposed to be haunted—if no one else does?"

"Yeah," said Timothy. "And he didn't even used to go here."

Titus looked at him in surprise. "He said he did."

"I know," replied Timothy. "But that's what I can't figure out. He was walking through the parking lot just now, and Mrs. Mason made him carry plants for her. But she didn't know him. She had to ask him what his name was."

"What was it?" asked Sarah-Jane.

"He said it was Dave."

"Well, maybe Dave used to go here, and Mrs.

Mason just doesn't remember him."

But Timothy shook his head. "You don't know Mrs. Mason. She knows everything there is to know about every kid who ever went here in the whole history of the world. And another thing. Why was he still hanging around? I thought he left just after we got here."

" 'Curiouser and curiouser,' " said Titus. (It was an expression he had picked up from *Alice in Wonderland,* and he liked it a lot.)

The three cousins were silent for a while, thinking all this over. Then suddenly, they heard a loud bang, as if someone had knocked something over.

They each stopped in the middle of what they were doing. They looked exactly like kids playing "statues" or "frozen tag."

"What was that?" whispered Sarah-Jane.

"Not ghosts. *Not* ghosts," said Timothy firmly. "Right?"

The other two nodded.

"OK, then. Let's go see what it was."

Sarah-Jane said, "Shouldn't we wait for Mr. Bender?"

"No," said Timothy, already at the door. "Because we don't know how long Mr. Bender will be gone, and whoever made the noise might get away." He was determined to settle this ghost business once and for all.

"I'm with Tim," said Titus.

The boys looked expectantly at Sarah-Jane. They didn't want to force her to come along if she didn't want to. But they didn't want to leave her out of things either.

They didn't have to worry. Sarah-Jane had no intention of being left out.

So the three cousins crept out into the hall.

They looked up and down.

There was no one there.

But the noise had seemed to come from the direction of the supply room, so they headed that way.

Suddenly Timothy, who was in the lead, held up his hand in warning. There were scuffling noises coming from the supply room.

Quickly the cousins opened the nearest classroom door and ducked behind it.

It was a good hiding place. No one who was

coming out of the supply room would be able to see them. The only problem was, *they* weren't able to see anything either.

So, as quietly as they could, they all snuck out from their hiding place and crept toward the supply room.

They had just reached it when Sarah-Jane gave a muffled little squeal and pointed down. Oozing out from under the door came a mysterious trickle of red.

That did it.

Once again the cousins spun around and fled down the hall. They burst into Room 208 in a breathless heap.

7
WHAT STUFF?

This time Mr. Bender wasn't there to comfort them, so it took them longer to calm down.

"What *was* that?" said Sarah-Jane at last.

"B-blood?" asked Titus.

It was what they were all thinking.

"Just like a horror movie," gulped Timothy. (He had watched a really gross one at a friend's house once, when he knew he wasn't allowed to. Now he sure wished he hadn't done that!)

Then Timothy happened to look over at the poster of the rugged mountain climbers, who meekly, determinedly kept on going. "We have to go back to the supply room," he said.

"WHAT?!" cried Titus and Sarah-Jane together.

"Yes," said Timothy. "Because if that stuff

really was blood, then maybe somebody's hurt and we have to get help. But if it's not blood—if it's some kind of trick, then we don't want it to work."

"What do you mean 'trick'?" asked Titus as they all took a deep breath and started back.

Sarah-Jane said, "I know. It's like in this book I read." She was trying to sound casual, but her words came out all fast and squeaky. "Anyway, in the book there was this spooky, old house. And there were mysterious lights at night—and weird noises and stuff. Only the house wasn't *really* haunted. There were these people who were looking for buried treasure in the basement. They made the lights and noises themselves to scare other people away. It was all just a trick."

And so was the red ooze.

"Tempera paint!" said Titus disgustedly when they took a close-up look.

They were so mad about being tricked that they forgot to be scared. Timothy boldly opened the door all the way, and the three of them stepped inside.

34

There was no one in the supply room. But there *was* a jar of red paint. It wasn't lying on the floor. It was standing right side up, only on the wrong shelf.

"Here's what I think," said Timothy. "I think someone poured a little bit of paint under the door on purpose. To scare us away."

Sarah-Jane agreed. "Yes, because if someone had knocked it over by accident, the jar would still be lying on the floor, and there would be paint all over the place. But who did it?"

"Dave!" said Timothy and Titus together.

Again Sarah-Jane agreed. "Yes! Because he's the only one who knew about the school being haunted. So maybe he made it all up in the first place. Just like in the book I read."

Titus nodded. "The question is, *why?*"

Suddenly Timothy realized what had bothered him earlier. "The book bag!" he cried.

Titus and Sarah-Jane stared at him.

"No, listen! Remember how heavy the book bag looked when Dave first told us not to go upstairs? Maybe he had something *in* there —something he stole."

Titus looked doubtful. "What? What's there to steal in here? Spelling books and construction paper?"

Timothy had to admit that Titus had a point. "I don't know. But whatever it was, he didn't have anything when I saw him again later— because that time he was tossing his bag around like it was nothing."

Titus said in his best detective voice, "OK. So this guy Dave has been sneaking in and out. When he leaves, his book bag is full and heavy. When he comes back, it's light and empty. So we figured it out. He's stealing things a little bit at a time and hiding them somewhere nearby—probably in that car! And he keeps coming back for more."

"More *what*?" asked Sarah-Jane. "We still haven't figured *that* out."

"More stuff," said Titus.

"More *what* stuff?" persisted Sarah-Jane.

"How do I know?" cried Titus, annoyed that he didn't know. "Just more . . . stuff. I mean, maybe they keep other things here in the storeroom besides textbooks and art supplies."

Timothy had been wandering farther into the room while Titus and Sarah-Jane discussed the case. Now his voice came to them from the other side of some shelves. "Hey, you guys! Come here! Quick! I've got it!"

8
TRAPPED!

Titus and Sarah-Jane rushed to join Timothy. Right away they saw what he meant.

The three of them had forgotten that a school didn't just have textbooks and paper. It also had—of course!—cassette players, calculators, VCR's. All sorts of electronic equipment.

And they saw something else. Empty spaces on the shelves.

"So *that's* it!" breathed Titus. "Dave has been stealing electronic stuff. He's been able to sneak in and out because there aren't that many people around yet."

"He sure doesn't want *us* around," said Sarah-Jane.

"Well, too bad for him," said Timothy. "The T.C.D.C. has cracked another case.

Come on. We have to tell Mr. Bender and Mrs. Mason what's been going on up here."

But they couldn't do that, because just then someone slammed the supply room door. They rushed to the door and tried to get out. But they were shut in.

Trapped.

"What's the matter with this doorknob?" cried Titus. "It won't turn! Hey, let us out! Somebody help! We're stuck in here!"

"Help, help!" cried Timothy and Sarah-Jane, pounding on the door. "Somebody, please help!"

9
THE SEARCH

After what seemed like a hundred hours (but what was really only a couple of minutes), they heard running footsteps. A grown-up's footsteps, and Mr. Bender's voice calling for them.

Suddenly the door was yanked open, and they tumbled out into the hall.

"What happened?" cried Mr. Bender. "There was a chair jammed under the doorknob!"

"Mr. Bender," gasped Timothy. "Did anyone pass you on the stairway just now?"

"No, but what—?"

"That means he's probably still up here!"

"Who?"

"Dave!"

"Who's Dave?"

Naturally, they all started talking at once. Mr.

Bender didn't try to make them take a deep breath and talk slowly. (Timothy was glad —he didn't think he could stand to be calm at a time like this.) But he did insist that only one of them could talk at a time. Since it was Timothy's school, Titus and Sarah-Jane picked him to do the talking.

Mr. Bender listened intently as Timothy rushed on with the story. "So anyway," Timothy concluded, "Dave scared us away with the paint trick. Then he snuck out with more stuff. Only, we didn't *stay* scared, and we came *back* to the supply room. Then, when Dave came back to get *more* electronic stuff, he must have heard us say we were going to get you and Mrs. Mason. So he shut us in the supply room so he could make his getaway. But right then you came back, so—"

"You think he's still up here somewhere?"

The three cousins nodded, holding their breath to hear what Mr. Bender would say.

He said, "OK. Tell you what. I'll stand guard at the head of the stairs, so he can't sneak out. And you three—the T.C.D.C., was it?—you check the classrooms. And yell as soon as you find him.''

The detective-cousins started with the classroom nearest to the supply room and the stairs. (They reasoned that Dave couldn't have gotten far when he heard Mr. Bender coming.)

Of course, the classroom *looked* empty, but they weren't too worried about that. They figured Dave would be hiding.

They were right.

After they had looked under the desks and behind the shelves, they found him. He was squeezed into the teacher's narrow coat closet.

Sarah-Jane rushed to get Mr. Bender.

Dave was hopping mad. He pushed past Titus and Timothy and bolted for the door, calling them names all the way.

But he didn't get very far.

Mr. Bender blocked the door and ushered him back into the classroom. Dave looked scared, but even with a teacher there, he still acted nasty.

''I don't know what you're talking about!'' he said when Mr. Bender asked him some questions. "I don't know anything about any supply room!"

"Oh, really?" said Titus. "Then how did you get fresh red tempera paint on your shoe?"

Dave looked down in alarm at his shoes. Then, without meaning to, he glanced nervously toward the window.

Sarah-Jane jumped up and ran to see what was out there. She saw the blue station wagon, still waiting in the parking lot. The teenage girl was still in the driver's seat.

"Who is that girl?" Sarah-Jane demanded of Dave.

He glared at her, but he answered, "My cousin."

Sarah-Jane put her hands on her hips. "Does she know what you're doing?"

Dave snorted. "Are you kidding? It was her idea."

Sarah-Jane was so shocked that anyone's girl cousin would think up such a thing, that she couldn't say a word.

But Mr. Bender said, "That means they probably haven't had time to take the equipment away, and we'll find it still in the car. We don't want Dave here warning her off. Timothy, run tell Mrs. Mason to get out to the parking lot. Don't let that girl get away. We'll come along behind you."

"Gotcha!" cried Timothy, speeding out the door.

THE BEST YET

When Dave and his cousin were trapped in the parking lot, they immediately started blaming each other. But Mrs. Mason cut them off. She had opened the back door of the station wagon and found the stolen equipment under some blankets. "How *dare* you!" she spluttered. "How *dare* you steal from Stevenson Elementary!"

Mr. Bender said, "I have a feeling Stevenson isn't the only school they've been stealing from. This is quite a little racket you've got going, isn't it?"

But Dave and his cousin didn't look ashamed of themselves. They just looked mad that they had been caught.

And that made Timothy mad. He said, "You

guys think you can do anything you want, don't you? You take stuff that doesn't belong to you. And you lie to people and scare them and shut them in supply rooms and call them names. You know what your problem is? You're not—you're not—*meek*!"

But even so, Timothy almost felt sorry for the thieves as Mrs. Mason marched them off toward her office. He shook his head sadly and said, "A fate worse than death."

Mr. Bender cleared his throat and said briskly, "Yes. Well. We still have some work to do in the room. How about it? Are you still interested?"

They certainly were.

In celebration of their detective work, Mr. Bender got them each a donut from the teachers' lounge. Then they went back to Room 208—which, for Timothy, was beginning to feel like home.

When it was time to leave, the cousins turned at the head of the stairway to wave good-bye to Mr. Bender. He smiled and called, "*Bienaventurados*! Good adventure to you!"

"You know what?" Timothy said to his cousins. "I think this is going to be my best year yet!"

The End